W9-AHY-929

SIMON & SCHUSTER BOOKS FOR YOUNG READERS
An imprint of Simon & Schuster Children's Publishing Division
1230 Avenue of the Americas, New York, New York 10020

For information about special discounts for bulk purchases, please contact Simon & Schuster Special Sales
at 1-866-506-1949 or business@simonandschuster.com.
The Simon & Schuster Speakers Bureau can bring authors to your live event. For more information
or to book an event, contact the Simon & Schuster Speakers Bureau at 1-866-248-3049
or visit our website at www.simonspeakers.com.
Book design by Laurent Linn
The text for this book was set in Family Dog.
The illustrations for this book were rendered in watercolor and ink.
Manufactured in China
0720 SCP
First Edition
2 4 6 8 10 9 7 5 3 1
Library of Congress Cataloging-in-Publication Data
Names: Wells, Rosemary, author, illustrator.
Title: Max & Ruby and the Babysitting Squad / Rosemary Wells.
Other titles: Max and Ruby and the Babysitting Squad
Description: First edition. | New York : Simon & Schuster Books for Young Readers, Paula Wiseman Books, [2020]
| Series: [A Max and Ruby adventure ; 2] | Audience: Ages 4–8. | Audience: Grades 2–3. |
Summary: Ruby and Louise create their own new Babysitting Squad business, but watching their first client,
Percy Wardropper, proves to be a challenge.
Identifiers: LCCN 2019053675 (print) | LCCN 2019053676 (eBook) |
ISBN 9781534463288 (hardcover) | ISBN 9781534463295 (eBook)
Subjects: CYAC: Babysitters—Fiction. | Brothers and sisters—Fiction. | Rabbits—Fiction.
Classification: LCC PZ7.W46843 Mard 2020 (print) | LCC PZ7.W46843 (eBook) | DDC [E]—dc23
LC record available at https://lccn.loc.gov/2019053675
LC eBook record available at https://lccn.loc.gov/2019053676

Max & Ruby and the BABYSITTING SQUAD

ROSEMARY WELLS

A Paula Wiseman Book
SIMON & SCHUSTER BOOKS FOR YOUNG READERS
New York London Toronto Sydney New Delhi

Max's sister, Ruby, made a big sign where everyone in town could see it.

Max wanted to babysit too.

"**No**, Max," said Ruby. "You're not professional."

"**No way** are you bonded, Max!" said Louise.

That night the telephone rang. "Hello?" said Ruby.

It was Louise.

"We have our first job!" said Louise.

"Mrs. Wardropper has a beauty
appointment tomorrow at nine.
She wants **US** to take care of Percy!"

Next morning Louise came early.
Ruby and Louise sped to number 12 Hickory Lane.
Max brought his Earth Mover equipment along.

"You'll have to play with those
in the backyard, Max," said Ruby.

Ding-dong! went the Wardroppers' doorbell.

Percy opened the door in a skunk costume.

"Hi!" said Ruby and Louise. "We're the **Babysitting Squad**!"

"Goody-bye!" said Percy.

“Say hello to Louise and Ruby, Percy!” said Mrs. Wardropper.

“I have skunk stink in my Outer Space Squirter!” said Percy.

Mrs. Wardropper gave Ruby and Louise the hairdresser's number in case of emergencies.

Then she was out the door.

"We brought **lots** of games!" said Ruby to Percy.

"How about dominoes?" asked Louise.

“Or let’s build a castle?” suggested Louise.

Percy said, “Skunks don’t play games.”

Then without another word, Percy vanished.

Ruby and Louise looked for Percy
behind the shades and in the cupboards.

Was Percy hiding under the bed or behind the castle?

They even looked for Percy in the shower.

"Where **is** he?" asked Louise.

"**Oh no!** Losing the baby on our first babysitting job!"

said Ruby.

"Here comes the **skunk stink**!"

said a voice from a heating vent.

It was Percy. A cloud of Vita-Mint Mouthwash filled the air.

"He must be in the attic!" said Ruby.

“Look out! I’m preparing **spider juice vapor!**” said Percy.

“Percy, **come down** for Chutes and Ladders!” said Louise.

“We can play the xylophone!” suggested Ruby.

Louise served up graham crackers with grape jelly.

"How about setting up the cowboy village, Percy?" said Louise.

Out of the heating vent puffed a cloud of Heavenly Man Aftershave.

Suddenly from outdoors came a noise
of rock crushing and electric zinging.

Max's Saw-toothed Dirt Bucketer and his Rock Crusher
were **clanging** and **banging** around the backyard.

Percy stood at an attic window,
looking down below at the backyard.

He saw it all.

"Want it!" Percy yelled.

Percy wanted to know how to work the Rock Crusher.

"**Don't** push the red button!" said Ruby.

But Percy **did** push the red button.

It went into the sling-and-fling gear.

Mrs. Wardropper came home.

"Oh no!" said Mrs. Wardropper. "I can't tell who's who!"

Max had an idea.

Max turned on the sprinkler so that
Mrs. Wardropper would feel better.